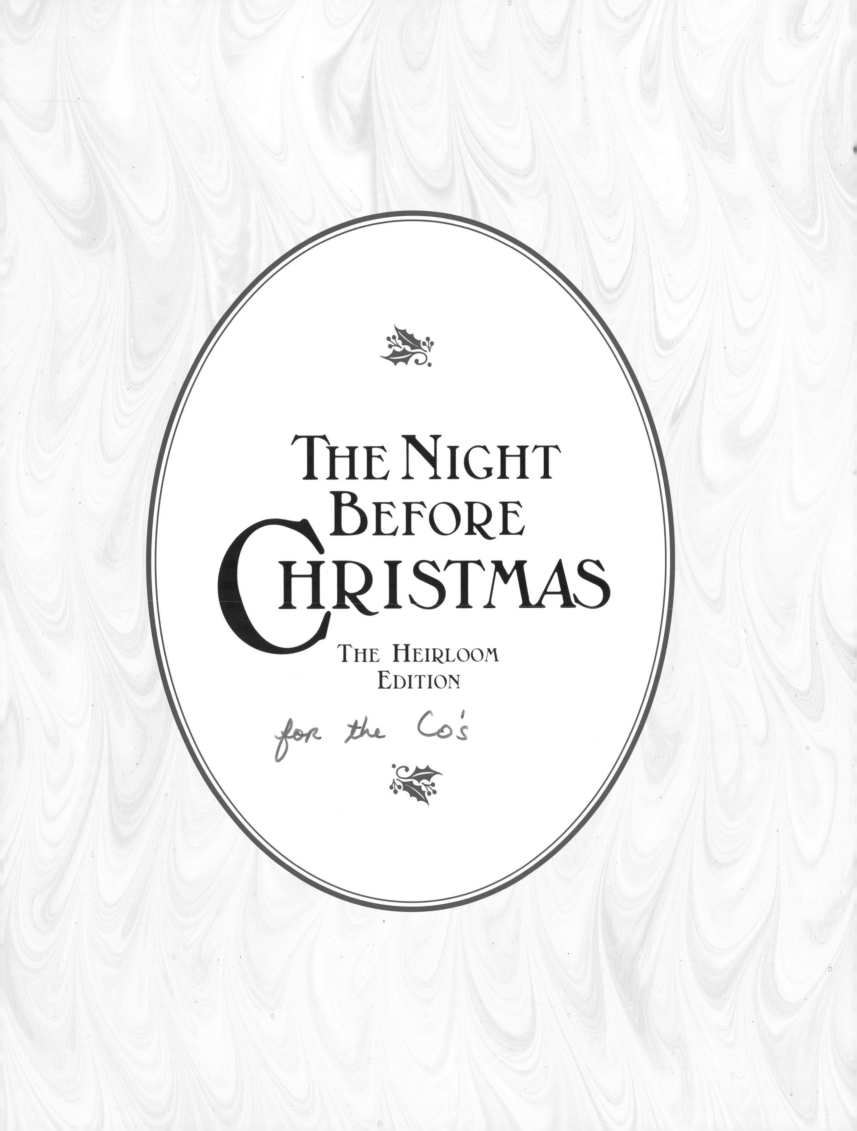

The Night Before Christmas

The Heirloom Edition

for the Co's

THE NIGHT BEFORE CHRISTMAS

THE HEIRLOOM EDITION

by Clement C. Moore

Illustrated by Christian Birmingham

RUNNING PRESS

PHILADELPHIA · LONDON

9   8   7   6   5   4   3   2
Digit on the right indicates the number of this printing

Library of Congress Cataloging-in-Publication Number 2001087017

ISBN 0-7624-1069-8

Designed by Bill Jones
Edited by Virginia Mattingly and Susan K. Hom
Typography: Milton

This book may be ordered by mail from the publisher.
Please include $2.50 for postage and handling.
But try your bookstore first!

Running Press Book Publishers
125 South Twenty-second Street
Philadelphia, Pennsylvania 19103-4399

Visit us on the web!
www.runningpress.com

INTRODUCTION

In 1822, a New York clergyman
named Clement Clarke Moore spun together
Christmas memories for his children. The poem he
wrote featured a red-suited Santa in a reindeer-drawn
sleigh, a never-empty sack of toys, and stockings hung
expectantly above the fireplace. He called it *A Visit from
St. Nicholas,* and it was then published anonymously in a
newspaper in Troy, New York. It captured the public's
imagination. The poem's opening line, "'Twas the night
before Christmas," soon replaced the original title.

One reason Moore's poem has endured is that it is a joy
to read aloud. Beginning in hushed suspense, the
poem builds to a dramatic crescendo as the rollicking
verses usher in the mysterious midnight visitor.

A tale of anticipation and wonder, *The Night Before
Christmas* has become a holiday tradition in itself
for many families. So as you open these pages,
whether for a first Christmas or to recall those
past, celebrate and share the timeless joys
of this enchanting holiday.

'T was the night
before Christmas,
when all through
the house
not a creature
was stirring,
not even a mouse;

The stockings were hung
by the chimney
with care,
In hopes that St. Nicholas
soon would be there.

The children were nestled
all snug in their beds,
While visions of sugarplums
danced in their heads;

And Mama
in her kerchief
and I in my cap,
Had just settled down
for a long winter's nap—

When out on the lawn
there rose such a clatter,
I sprang from my bed
to see what was the matter.

Away to the window
I flew like a flash,
Tore open the shutters
and threw up the sash.

The moon on the breast
of the new-fallen snow,
Gave a luster of midday
to objects below;

When, what
to my wondering eyes
should appear,
But a miniature sleigh
and eight tiny
reindeer,

With a little old driver
so lively and quick,
I knew in a moment
it must be St. Nick.

More rapid than eagles
his coursers they came,
And he whistled, and shouted,
and called them by name—

"Now, Dasher! Now, Dancer!
Now, Prancer and Vixen!
On, Comet! On, Cupid!
On, Donder and Blitzen!

To the top of the porch,
to the top of the wall!
Now, dash away!
Dash away!
Dash away all!"

As dry leaves before
the wild hurricane fly,
When they meet
with an obstacle,
mount to the sky,

So up to the housetop
the coursers they flew,
With sleigh full of toys–
and St. Nicholas too;

And then in a twinkling,
I heard on the roof
The prancing and pawing
of each little hoof.

As I drew in my head
and was turning around,
Down the chimney
St. Nicholas came
with a bound.

He was dressed all in fur
from his head to his foot,
And his clothes
were all tarnished
with ashes and soot.

A bundle of toys
he had flung on his back,
And he looked like a peddler
just opening his pack.

His eyes how they twinkled!
His dimples how merry!
His cheeks were like roses,
his nose like a cherry!

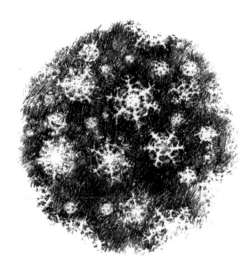

His droll little mouth
was drawn up like a bow,
And the beard on his chin
was as white as the snow!

The stump of a pipe
he held tight in his teeth.
And the smoke it encircled
his head like a wreath.

He had a broad face
and a little round belly
That shook when he laughed
like a bowl full of jelly.

He was chubby and plump—
a right jolly old elf,
And I laughed
when I saw him,
in spite of myself.

A wink of his eye
and a twist of his head,
Soon gave me to know
I had nothing to dread.

He spoke not a word,
but went straight to his work,
And filled all the stockings
then turned with a jerk,

And laying his finger
aside of his nose,
And giving a nod,
up the chimney he rose.

He sprang to his sleigh,
to his team gave a whistle,
And away they all flew
like the down of a thistle.

But I heard him exclaim
as he drove out of sight,
"Merry Christmas to all
and to all a Good Night!"